Carolina Medical Assessment Center

2735 Speissegger Dr. Suite 107

North Charleston, SC 29405

The Adventures of Little Chick

Photograph taken by Thomas Shelby

Paul Evans lives in Laurel, Mississippi. His great love for reading books at a young age led him to try his skills at writing. He views his writing as just a hobby for now. Paul's hope for the future is to turn his gift into a full-time occupation. *The Adventures of Little Chick* is his third book to be published, and he plans to write a couple of sequels to *Little Chick*. He uses animated characters that take on real-life characteristics and situations with the intent to illuminate the joys of sharing with and caring for others.

Paul is shown here with his two year old granddaughter, Akurya,(Kee Kee). She shows great interest in books and having stories read to her at this early age.

The Adventures of
of
Little Chick

By

Paul Evans

Illustrated by
Laura Robinson

Coastal Publishing, Inc.
1025-C West 5th North Street
Summerville, SC 29483

Library of Congress Cataloging-in-Publication Data

Evans, Paul, 1950-
  The adventures of Little Chick / by Paul Evans ;
illustrated by Laura Robinson.-- 1st ed.
  p. cm.
  SUMMARY: Little Chick was curious, perhaps too
curious for his own good. When Little Chick gets lost,
Mr. Field Mouse and his friends try to help Little Chick
find his way home--but will Mr. Hawk spoil their
efforts?
  Audience: Elementary grades
  ISBN 0-9705727-7-8

  1. Chickens--Juvenile fiction. 2. Mice--Juvenile
fiction. 3. Hawks--Juvenile fiction. [1. Chickens--
Fiction. 2. Mice--Fiction. 3. Hawks--Fiction.]
I. Robinson, Laura, 1973-ill. II. Title.

PZ7.E89226Adv 2001   [E]
                        QBI01-700353

Inspired by

a desire to share my gift with others so that they may enjoy exciting and pleasurable reading.

Dedicated to

my family, my friends, and the readers who support and believe in me.

Foreword

Little Chick's curiosity leads him on a wild and scary adventure. Mr. Field Mouse, along with some friends, try to help Little Chick find his way back home. The mean old Mr. Hawk tries to spoil their efforts.

Contents

The Adventures
of
Little Chick

One

Catching Worms

Early one spring morning, as the sun leaped over the horizon and turned the gray sky blue, you could smell the sweetness of the honeysuckle as a cool breeze of moist air blew gently over the meadow.

In the far distance you could hear the cows as they began to graze. You could also hear a distant rooster crow as he stood atop an old rickety fence.

Mother Hen was up early that

morning, scratching in the earth, trying to find food for her newborn chicks. After enough worms were collected, she hurried back into the nest to feed her babies. They quickly ate all she had and cried for more.

Mother Hen rushed back into the yard to find more food for their hungry bellies. She scratched around in the earth once more. After several minutes, she reached down and pulled up several large worms, enough to finish feeding her little chicks. As she started back, Mother Hen could hear the babies crying, "Cheep, cheep, cheep, cheep."

One of the baby chicks had been watching his mother gather food. This looked exciting to him so he decided to go out and help. After several tries he finally managed to get out of the nest. He fell face down on his beak, then cried "Cheep, cheep, cheep, cheep."

Mother Hen heard his cries and rushed over to him. "Oh! Oh! Little Chick!" she called him. "What are you doing out of the nest? You must be careful and never do this again. Some mean old hawk might fly down from the sky and carry you away, and I'll never see you again." She gathered him up and carried him back to the nest to continue with her feeding.

"Cheep, cheep, cheep, cheep," cried Little Chick, because he did not want to go back into the nest.

After all the babies had been fed, they snuggled close to Mother Hen and fell silently to sleep.

While Little Chick slept, he dreamed of catching lots and lots of worms.

Little Chick awakened and found everyone else still fast asleep, so he decided to sneak out of the nest once more and catch himself a worm.

He managed to hop and wobble to the spot where he had seen his mother digging. "This is the place," said Little Chick. He scratched around in the dirt with his tiny feet. Suddenly he saw this big worm crawl from underneath the dirt. "Cheep, cheep!" shouted Little Chick as he bravely grabbed the big worm with his tiny beak. The worm was much too big for him to hold, and it slipped away.

Little Chick leaped upon the worm once again, and the worm began to crawl back into the hole. Little Chick was holding him by the tail and pulled him out of the hole again. The worm was still much too strong, and they pulled back and forth. Little Chick tightly held on. He dug his feet into the ground and pulled and pulled and pulled. Suddenly the worm slipped away from him and disappeared into the ground.

Little Chick tumbled backward and rolled over and over again because he had been pulling so hard. He rolled through a hole in the fence and right out into the open field.

"Cheep," he said, as he tried to get to his feet. He shook the dirt and straw from his tiny little feathers.

"Oh! How did I get here?" he said. He did not see himself go through the hole in the fence because he was too busy tumbling over.

As far as Little Chick's eyes could see, there was a golden field of soft wheat, waving in the gentle breeze like an ocean of yellow water, and there was just as much blue sky above him. Everything seemed much bigger out here in the open. It was frightening. This was the first time that he had seen anything beyond the little fenced-in yard around his home.

"I did not see this place in my dream when I was trying to catch a worm, nor have I seen it from inside my nest," said Little Chick.

Two

Crossing the Pond

As he stared into the big blue sky, Little Chick could see a strange black dot floating beneath the fluffy white clouds. This really excited Little Chick. Oh, how he wished that he could float beneath the clouds like this strange object.

Suddenly this tiny black dot became bigger and bigger until it was upon Little Chick so fast he hardly had time to move out of its reaches.

"Cheep, cheep, cheep, cheep," he cried, as he scurried frantically trying to find his way back home. He realized that this strange thing that had swooped down upon him must have been the mean old hawk his mother had told him to be aware of, always.

When Little Chick finally stopped running, he was deep into the field of soft golden wheat. He looked up and could still see mean old Mr. Hawk. His wings were long and still as he floated around in circles looking for Little Chick.

"What's wrong, little fellow? Why are you running so fast?" said a squeaky friendly voice from inside the wheat field.

"That mean old Mr. Hawk is trying to catch me. I think he wants to eat me," cried Little Chick.

"Now, now, don't cry. I'll help you. You can stay here with me until he leaves, and then I'll help you get home. You're not the only one that he chases. He's tried to catch me many times. Where do you live?" asked Mr. Field

Mouse, as he stepped through the golden wheat.

He was a very old and wise-looking field mouse. He was fat and round and wore thick wire-framed glasses and a bright red coat, blue trousers, and gray shoes.

"I am lost. Please help me get back home to my mother and my sisters and brothers." Little Chick cried and cried.

Mr. Field Mouse said, "There is a family just like the one you just described that just might be your family. They live on the other side of the pond. I'll take you there, but first we must find a way to get across. It is much too dangerous to try to go around."

After hearing their conversation, Mr. Frog leaped out of the pond, dripping wet, and said, "I will help you get Little Chick across the pond, Mr. Field Mouse. After all, you two are not the only ones that Mr. Hawk has tried to catch and eat. I will gather some lily pads to float on, and you two can bring some wheat straw to paddle the pads across."

After gathering the wheat straw and lily pads they climbed aboard and proceeded to cross the pond.

The water was cool and very still. Little Chick sat calmly upon the lily pads while Mr. Frog and Mr. Field Mouse used the wheat straw to paddle them forward.

Just as they reached the other side Mr. Frog stopped paddling and hopped off to help the others get ashore.

Suddenly there was a big splash in the water just behind the lily pads where Mr. Mouse and Little Chick sat. They almost fell into the water.

"Hold on!" shouted Mr. Frog. "We have awakened Mr. Catfish, and he must be very hungry this morning.

Mr. Mouse, give me your hand, and I'll quickly pull you to shore. Little Chick," he said, "hold on to Mr. Mouse's tail very tight."

Mr. Frog pulled and pulled. Suddenly the water erupted once more and up popped Mr. Catfish. He took a huge bite out of the lily pads just as Little Chick was jerked ashore.

"That was very close," said Mr. Field Mouse.

"Yes, we made it just in time," said Mr. Frog.

This side of the pond looked different from the golden wheat field on the other side. It was filled with tall trees and thick bushes. It looked very dangerous to Little Chick.

Mr. Frog said, "I must leave you now and get back to the pond. Just remember to stay close and be careful because these woods are filled with all kinds of strange animals that might try to eat you for breakfast."

They thanked Mr. Frog and started off through the woods.

Three

Snake in the Grass

Mr. Field Mouse stopped and said, "Look there, Little Chick, through the opening in the woods. See that big tall monster with his four arms spinning round and round?"

"Yes," answered Little Chick shivering. "What is that?"

Mr. Field Mouse said, "That is a windmill on a farm. Just below the windmill is where the family that I told you about lives."

"But that doesn't look like where I came from," said Little Chick.

"Well," said Mr. Mouse, "let's go and see."

From behind Mr. Field Mouse came a hissing and rattling sound. He turned suddenly and saw Mr. Rattlesnake beaming down upon him with fire-red eyes and a long black lashing tongue.

"Hello there, my friend, Mr. Field Mouse. What are you doing in my neck of the woods, and who is your friend? Come closer and let's talk," said Mr. Rattlesnake. "No!" shouted Mr. Mouse, as he backed away. "You're not my friend. You're just another snake in the grass. And knowing you, I know that you are up to no good." Mr. Snake leaped forward, striking fiercely at Mr. Mouse.

Mr. Mouse ducked just in time and ran swiftly away. He called out nervously, "Run, Little Chick. You know our destination. If I am lucky enough to get away from Mr. Snake, I'll circle around and meet you there."

Little Chick ran hastily down the trail and through the opening in the woods and on to the windmill on the farm. Soon Mr. Mouse joined him, and they were horrified at what they saw. The little chicken house where a family once lived was torn completely apart. Feathers were all over the yard. There was a trail of feathers leading around to the other side of the windmill and into the woods.

Squeaky Mouse, who lived on the farm, appeared from underneath a pile of straw. He told them that the mean fox had sneaked onto the farm that morning just before the sun came up and had taken the poor, helpless family of chickens, who were still fast asleep in their nest, away with him.

"Oh what must I do? There are so many dangers out here in the world. I'll never find my family again," cried Little Chick.

Squeaky Mouse with his small, black, beaded eyes and long, pointed tail scurried back underneath his pile of straw. He called out, "You must leave here at once before Mr. Fox returns. He always comes here to steal his food, and you don't want to be here when he returns."

Brokenhearted, tired, and hungry, Little Chick and Mr. Field Mouse continued on around the edge of the woods in search of Little Chick's family.

It began to rain, so they hurried into the woods to seek shelter underneath a big black tree all covered with gray hanging moss. It rained harder and harder! The wind blew, the thunder rolled, and the lightning struck down upon them. Mr. Mouse and Little Chick snuggled close together in a hollow at the foot of the big tree. There they stayed for two days, unable to continue their journey. Little Chick weeped constantly.

On the third day they awakened, still hungry but not so tired. The rain had stopped, and the sun was just rolling over the horizon.

Birds chirped, and the bees began to gather pollen from the honeysuckles. A cool breeze blew across the wheat field drying tiny drops of water from the straw that had been left there by the rain.

As Mr. Mouse peered out of the woods and across the golden field, he said "Why don't you come back to the wheat field and live with me, Little Chick? We have survived the dangers of the wilderness together. I know that we can live there in peace and harmony. Maybe one day if we're lucky, we will find your family."

Little Chick agreed to go and live with Mr. Mouse since he was all alone in the world and could not care for himself yet.

They did not go back across the pond. Instead, they built a home near the woods where they had been forced to seek shelter from the storm.

Four

Home Again

Days turned to weeks, and weeks turned to months. Mr. Mouse and Little Chick had lived together and enjoyed their little wheat straw house in harmony. Little Chick took on most of the chores around the house while Mr. Mouse went out daily to gather food. The both of them constantly thought of finding Little Chick's family. They took evening strolls throughout the wheat field looking for clues that might lead them to Chick's home and family. They could not venture out too far because Mr. Hawk was still very actively up to no good.

Twice he almost caught them while they were away from the comfort and safety of their little straw castle. Throughout the land, autumn had finally settled upon all that lived in this part of the country. The trees in the woods had begun to shed their once green, now gold, brown, and bronze-colored leaves.

The bees had stopped the gathering of pollen because the honeysuckles and sweet flowers were long gone.

Most of the birds and other animals had moved on to new ground.

Farmers began to harvest the wheat throughout the fields.

Mr. Hawk pulled daily raids upon the animals that were being forced to move because of harvest time.

"Wake up! Wake up!" shouted Mr. Mouse, one gray and windy morning. "Wake up, Little Chick, we must leave at once!"

27

Little Chick awakened to the sound of heavy machinery all around him. He could hardly hear the cries of Mr. Mouse.

"There is no time to waste. We must go at once!" shouted Mr. Mouse.

So they dashed out of the house and across the freshly cut opened field.

As the big machines rolled across the field, every few yards or so, they would chew up the wheat straw and spit out a bale.

Mr. Mouse and Little Chick ran from one bale to another, trying to get as far away as they could without being out the open field for too long.

They looked back once more, just in time to see their lovely little home being chewed up and spit out, from underneath the big machine.

Suddenly, there were huge wings flapping and sharp claws piercing upon them. In all this commotion, Little Chick heard Mr. Field Mouse cry out. "Run, Little Chick, run!" His voice rapidly faded away, upward into the clouds.

Mr. Hawk had finally captured Mr. Field Mouse and carried him away.

Little Chick weeped openly. "Cheep, cheep, cheep! Good-bye, Mr. Field Mouse, good-bye."

Little Chick felt lost and all alone once again. He loved and depended on Mr. Mouse and did not know how he would face the world on his own. But he knew that he could, because Mr. Mouse had taught him so much about life and survival.

So Little Chick set out on a journey of his own, in search of his family. He survived, day by day, sleeping in dark lonely places, scarcely finding enough food to fill his hungry stomach.

One day as he was going in no certain direction, he came upon a familiar-looking place. It was a little fenced-in yard with a little red chicken house sitting out in the middle of it, just like the one he had left so long ago.

Moments later he saw his mother. She was wearing a blue bonnet upon her head and a white apron tied around her waist. Mother Hen walked across the yard and scratched into the dirt. She moved a few steps further and scratched again, reached down, and plucked out several worms to eat. Little Chick's eyes filled with tears of joy. He shouted, "Mother! Mother! Is that you? Oh Mother! Mother! I am so glad to be home with you and the family again."

Mother Hen heard his cries and looked up in amazement to see Little Chick standing there all grown up. She screamed! "Little Chick! Little Chick! Welcome home, Little Chick! It's been such a long time! My, my, how you have grown!"

Little Chick hopped over the fence and embraced his mother. They stood and talked for what seemed like hours. He told her all about his adventures with Mr. Field Mouse and how Mr. Hawk had swooped down upon them and carried Mr. Field Mouse away into the clouds.

After Little Chick told his mother of his adventures, she said, "Son, you have been places and done things that I have never dreamed. Little Chick, you were destined to be adventurous, just like your father, Big Red Rooster, whom you resemble very much. He left us just weeks before you and your brothers and sisters were born. I still remember him, tall and handsome, and dressed in his long black split-tailed coat and black string necktie.

"Every morning at six o'clock he would go out and sit atop the old rickety fence and chat with all the other roosters from across the fields and valleys. 'Cock-a-do-la-do,' they would echo one to the other. He went out one morning, and I haven't seen him since. Maybe he just left on his own, maybe the farmer took him, or maybe the old fox got him. I don't know."

"Little Chick," said Mother Hen, "it is time for you to settle down and raise a family of your own and teach them the ways of life through your experiences. I am just an old hen now and can no longer care for you. You will have to continue on your own. Your brothers and sisters are still close by. They all have families of their own now."

Little Chick decided to live close to his mother, also, so that he could help protect and provide for her. And that's where he stayed . . . forever.

To Be Continued . . .